CAN YOU SAVE AN ENDANGERED SPECIES?

AN INTERACTIVE ECO ADVENTURE

BY ERIC BRAUN

CAPSTONE PRESS
a capstone imprint

You Choose Books are published by Capstone Press, an imprint of Capstone.
1710 Roe Crest Drive
North Mankato, Minnesota 56003
www.capstonepub.com

**Library of Congress Cataloging-in-Publication data is available on the Library
of Congress website.**
ISBN: 978-1-4966-9598-7 (library binding)
ISBN: 978-1-4966-9706-6 (paperback)
ISBN: 978-1-9771-5395-1 (eBook PDF)

Summary: Go on an adventure to try to save an endangered species! You can go to
Asia to protect elephants, travel to Africa to reintroduce scimitar-horned oryxes
into the wild, or trek to Central America to protect frogs from a deadly fungus!

Photo Credits
Alamy: Anton Sorokin, 91, BIOSPHOTO, 6; Capstone Press, 106-107;
Dreamstime/Tanisorn, 83; Getty Images: FACHROZI AMRI/Stringer, 25,
NurPhoto/Contributor, 39; Minden Pictures/Bert Willaert, 79; ScienceSource/E.
Hanumantha Rao, 17; Shutterstock: K Haney CHDPhoto, cover (top), 1 (t),
ChooChin, 94, GizmoPhoto, 47, k.z, 59, Lighttraveler, 42, marekuliasz, 68, Oleg
Mayorov, 63, PARITNTUB, 53, Rafal Cichawa, cover (bottom), backcover (t), 1
(b), 4, 104-105, Rich Carey, 100, Sam DCruz, 32, steve estvanik, 10, Teo Tarras,
35, Vaclav Sebak, 72, Wildceylon31, 21

Design Elements:
Shutterstock/tonia_tkach

Editorial Credits
Editor: Mandy Robbins; Designer: Bobbie Nuytten; Media Researcher:
Kelly Garvin; Production Specialist: Katy LaVigne

TABLE OF CONTENTS

ABOUT YOUR ADVENTURE

YOU are a researcher trying to save endangered species around the world from extinction. With your team of dedicated scientists, can you help save them before it's too late?

Chapter One sets the scene. Then you choose which path to read. Follow the directions at the bottom of the page as you read the stories. The decisions you make will change your outcome. After you finish one path, go back and read the others for new perspectives and more adventures.

Turn the page to begin your adventure.

CHAPTER 1

ENDANGERED SPECIES BIOLOGIST

YOU walk along a crowded city sidewalk on a beautiful summer day. You pass a stand where a man is selling soft drinks and hot pretzels that smell delicious. Up ahead, you see the double doors that lead into the research lab where you'll be meeting new coworkers. A surge of excitement runs through you.

You are an endangered species biologist, and it's your first day on the job. You will be working to restore endangered species. You're about to join a team made up of some of the best scientists in the business.

Turn the page.

7

One of these scientists greets you in the lobby. She has dark hair piled up in a neat bun and a warm smile. She introduces herself as Dr. Moua.

"But you can call me Alana," she says. "We'll be working together. Let me show you around." As she shakes your hand, you notice that her earrings are tiny enamel frogs.

Alana shows you around a zoo with cheetahs, lions, black-footed ferrets, and other animals. You also get to see a lab and a library. Then you make your way to a conference room to meet the rest of the team. Everyone takes a seat. The leader of the team, Dr. Jones, tells you about its mission. The team has projects all over the world studying species diversity and conservation. The researchers make recommendations to better protect and support species.

Dr. Jones describes three projects that need help right now. In the first project, you would be facing off against elephant poachers in Myanmar. The second involves reintroducing a type of desert antelope called the scimitar-horned oryx into the grasslands of Chad. This was their last-known natural habitat. The third is a project in Panama to save frogs from a deadly fungus.

You and Alana will join one of these missions. You ask her which one she prefers, but she says, "You choose."

To fight against elephant poaching in Myanmar, turn to page 11.

To work with oryxes in Chad, turn to page 43.

To work to save frogs in Panama, turn to page 73.

CHAPTER 2

ELEPHANTS IN MYANMAR

Scientists have been working in Myanmar for decades to learn about Asian elephants. Due to poaching, habitat loss, and conflicts with humans, these elephants are severely threatened. Only 30,000 to 50,000 remain in the wild. You can't resist the chance to work with these majestic animals up close.

So you tell Alana, "Let's go to Myanmar."

Myanmar lies in Southeast Asia, just to the west of China and Thailand. Your flight takes two days and one long layover in Taiwan. When you finally step outside the airport, you are hit by a wall of heat and humidity. It's 100 degrees, and the air feels as sticky as glue.

Turn the page.

By the time you meet with a team of researchers at the lab, you are hot, exhausted, and uncomfortable—yet still energized by the job that lies ahead of you.

One of the research leaders is Dr. Charlie Poole, a tall, strong man in shorts and sandals. While you sit in his small, cramped office, he explains the two main missions of the facility. One is to stop poaching.

"It's illegal to kill elephants," Charlie says, clicking his ballpoint pen in frustration. "But some people—they don't care."

Poachers used to only hunt male elephants so they could sell their ivory tusks. But in recent years, poachers are also selling the elephants' skin and meat. That means females are being poached as well as males, which can more quickly lead to extinction for these animals.

The other main mission is learning how elephants move across the land, how often they use certain parts of the land, and how far they roam.

"With increased tourism in the country, it's especially important to get a handle on their habits," Charlie says. Researchers want to help make sure that elephants and humans can live peacefully in the same areas.

The main way researchers track elephants is by putting tracking collars on them. They use GPS satellites to follow the animals' movements. A crew will be leaving first thing in the morning to search for elephants and attach collars. Charlie says you can be part of that expedition. You are already thinking about how nice it will be to go to your hotel and sleep until morning.

Turn the page.

"But we also have a more pressing mission," he says. "We've had a report of poachers in a remote region of the forest. We're going to send out a crew to stop them—right now."

To skip the mission and go to your hotel, go to the next page.

To head out to face the poachers, turn to page 19.

You wake up in the morning feeling refreshed and excited to get to work. You meet Alana for an early breakfast at an outdoor tea shop. The street is already crowded with people walking, riding bikes, and chatting with one another as they go about their business.

You are enjoying a bowl of mohinga, a fish stew with rice noodles, when a man sits down to join you. He has a scruffy beard, and his eyes are dark under the broad rim of his sun hat. You recognize him from the group you met at work yesterday.

"I'm Kan," he says, offering his hand. After you and Alana introduce yourselves, he says, "You better finish up. We're meeting two mahouts."

He explains that mahouts are local people who spend their lives working with elephants in the forest. They know many of the elephants and develop lifelong bonds with them.

Turn the page.

You finish your breakfast and head out with Kan. Soon, the three of you are racing through the forest in a little Jeep with no top. Kan is hollering over the wind and the sound of the engine.

"We've been collaring elephants since 2014," he tells you. "The information we get from them is critical. Elephants are losing their habitats, and as a result, they're coming into conflict with humans more often. The more we learn, the more we can do to protect them."

Beside you in the back seat and on the floor are several collars—big canvas straps with a box about the size of a couple bars of soap. Kan tells you the box contains technology like that in a smartphone. It sends GPS signals to satellites so that the elephant wearing the collar can be tracked.

Male elephants engage with one another.
The one on the right wears a tracking collar.

"But before we can track them, we have to
find them," Kan says. "The mahouts can help."

Turn the page.

At last, Kan stops the Jeep in a small village. Two men in ball caps come up and shake hands with Kan. He tells you that Ko and Win are mahouts here to help. Win begins speaking quickly to Kan in Burmese. Kan responds, and after a minute he turns to you.

"Win says that some elephants went through a farmer's home near here last night. They wrecked one of the buildings. They've also seen smashed foliage off the trail up ahead that might be evidence of elephants passing."

You can go talk to the farmer to learn about the elephants that wrecked his property, or you can follow the trail.

To talk with the farmer, turn to page 22.
To follow the tracks through the woods, turn to page 24.

You and Alana follow Charlie to his old, yellow pickup truck. Alana sits up front, while you take the back seat. With Charlie behind the wheel, you drive into the forest. A second truck with two more researchers follows you. Looking behind you, you notice that Charlie has a rifle in the back seat.

It takes almost two hours to reach the village where an elephant was recently killed nearby. Charlie talks to some villagers, who point him toward a path. You follow it deep into the woods. Charlie carries the rifle. Eventually, you come to a small section of matted leaves.

"See those leaves?" Charlie asks. "That's where the poacher spent the night. They call it nature's sleeping bag."

Turn the page.

You keep walking. The trail narrows, and you cross a small stream. After a while you emerge from the woods into a wide field. Before you step away from the trees, everyone stops. About 100 yards away, an elephant is eating grass. You look at it through binoculars. It has long tusks. It's a beautiful animal.

Suddenly it tips its head toward you. Its ears twitch.

"It senses us," Alana whispers.

"Yes," Charlie says. "But we're downwind, so the elephant doesn't smell us. It hasn't seen us."

No sooner than Charlie get the words out of his mouth, the elephant turns toward you. It begins charging. What do you do?

To run into the woods, turn to page 27.

To stay where you are and use a tranquilizer, turn to page 29.

Ko and Alana crowd into the back of the Jeep with you, while Win and Kan sit up front. Win points out directions. Within a few minutes, you arrive at the farm. The farmer steps out of his home to meet you. His two young children peer at you from inside.

The farmer walks toward a field. There, a small outbuilding has been destroyed—a wall is knocked over, the floor is broken up, and the thatched roof has collapsed. The farmer tells Kan that two elephants were eating the rice he had stored in the building yesterday. He scared them off by firing his gun into the air. When they ran away, one of them ran through this area.

Kan relays the story to you, and you watch the farmer closely. Though the elephants are gone, he still seems distracted. You remember his family hiding inside the house.

"What is he worried about?" you ask.

Kan asks the farmer, who doesn't say anything. But Ko and Win press him. Eventually, the farmer admits that a poacher had been here earlier in the day. He was asking about the elephants.

"The farmer says he didn't tell them anything," Kan says. "He believes in protecting the elephants, even though they can hurt his farming operation."

"We need to stop that poacher," Alana says.

"The poachers will be armed and possibly unfriendly," Kan says, "It may be wiser to focus on getting collars onto the elephants," Kan says. "The success of the program depends on it."

Kan and Alana both look to you for your opinion on what to do next.

To go after the poacher, turn to page 31.
To follow the tracks of the elephants, turn to page 35.

The farm is several miles away, and the elephants were last seen there a day ago. There's no reason to think they're still in the area. You'll have better luck following the tracks here.

Ko and Win lead you through broken branches and ripped leaves. After a while, the trail goes cold. You're starting to think you won't find an elephant today when Ko and Win stop. Ko holds out a hand to tell the group to wait.

You look over his shoulder and see a male elephant up ahead. Kan unshoulders his rifle and asks you for the tranquilizer. The drug is powerful enough to put an elephant to sleep, but just touching it would kill a human. So you are extra careful as you pass the tranquilizer shell.

Kan fires the dart, and the elephants staggers and lays down. You gasp.

"He'll be fine," Kan assures you.

A veterinarian removes a tranquilizer dart from the flesh of an elephant.

Alana opens up her pack and takes out one of the collars. The rest of you gather around the great beast. It is sleeping soundly.

Kan, Ko, and Win get the collar around the elephant's massive neck.

Turn the page.

That night, back at the facility, the team follows all the tagged elephants on a GPS-linked computer. There are at least 20 of them. Kan points to one of the dots on the map.

"That's the big fella from today!" Kan exclaims.

Everyone feels great about the successful day. You can't wait to get out there again tomorrow.

THE END

To read another adventure, turn to page 9.
To learn more about endangered species, turn to page 101.

"Run!" you yell.

You all dash into the woods, hoping the trees will slow the elephant down. Charlie and Alana start climbing a tree. You find a tree with a low branch and grab on. You lift yourself up and keep climbing. The elephant is getting close enough that you can feel vibrations coming from the ground and into the tree. You scramble higher.

The elephant crashes into Alana's tree. She falls to the ground. It rears up and gives a terrifying trumpet. Alana screams. So do you. You hope your scream will distract the elephant, but it doesn't.

The trees rattle and crack. Finally, sensing that your group is no longer a threat, the elephant tromps away. Alana is on the ground breathing heavily. Charlie is climbing down from his tree. The elephant is lumbering away across the field.

Turn the page.

"Alana!" you say. "Are you okay?"

She groans. "Ugh," she says. "I think I broke my ankle in the fall, but it could have been a lot worse."

"We better get you to a hospital," Charlie says.

Alana's ankle is swollen, and she's obviously in a lot of pain. But she's smiling with relief.

"Yeah," you say. "You were very, very lucky."

THE END

To read another adventure, turn to page 9.
To learn more about endangered species, turn to page 101.

"Quick!" you shout. "Let's trank it!"

Charlie takes his rifle from his shoulder, and you hand him the tranquilizer shell. You can't believe how calm he is as he loads it.

Come on, come on, come on, you think. *Hurry up!*

Just when you're about to turn and run for your life, Charlie fires the tranquilizer. The elephant stops in its tracks, stunned. It falls to one knee, then collapses onto its side. You can see its chest rise and fall as it breathes peacefully.

"Give me a collar," Charlie says.

With shaking hands, you reach into Alana's backpack and pull out one of the big collars. The three of you work together to wrap the collar around the elephant's neck and fasten it.

Turn the page.

You hide in the woods while Charlie gives the elephant a drug to wake it up. Its eyes flicker open as Charlie pets it gently. Twenty minutes later, the elephant has walked away.

"Unbelievable," Alana whispers.

"Come on, " Charlie says. "We need to find those poachers before they find any elephants."

You continue through the woods, following signs that the elephants have been by—broken branches, piles of dung. Near dusk, you are all tired and hungry as you return to the village. You are feeling bad that you didn't find the poachers. Suddenly you see some men climbing out of a Land Cruiser on the road near your Jeep. Inside their truck you can see a rack with two big rifles—really big. Rifles big enough to kill an elephant.

To question the men, turn to page 37.
To follow the men from a distance, turn to page 39.

Collars won't help the elephants if poachers are out there hunting them.

"We can collar the elephants tomorrow," you say, "Today we have to stop these poachers."

Kan nods. "You're right," he says. He speaks in Burmese to the farmer to get more information about the poacher. As the farmer describes the man who came to his farm, Ko gets excited. He says something quickly to Kan.

"Ko thinks he knows this man," Kan tells you and Alana. "We'll go to his home."

Kan thanks the farmer, and you pile back into the Jeep. You drive to the next village, which is beside a muddy lake. A woman is selling fruit at a stand under a pink umbrella you as you drive down the rutted dirt road. All the homes are built up on stilts to keep them dry during the rainy season.

Turn the page.

Ko points to a small wooden house up ahead. Two men sit on the porch under a thatched roof out front, watching you carefully as you pull up. You all get out of the Jeep and approach the men. Kan calls out to them in Burmese, but the men remain silent. Kan repeats himself. Ko adds a stern comment.

"Be calm, everyone," Kan says to the team in the jeep.

Finally the men invite you up to the porch. Kan asks them a few questions while you and Alana peek around. But the men do not invite you inside. You notice an elephant gun inside the window. As Kan continues to question them, the men start to get angry. One of them stands up. He has a pistol in his belt.

"Let's get out of here," Alana says.

Turn the page.

Kan raises his hands up and gives the men a big smile as he backs away. You hurry down the steps and back to the Jeep. The men watch you every step of the way.

After you drop Ko and Win at their village, you ask Kan what's will happen to the poachers.

"They had an elephant gun," you say.

"It's not enough. We didn't see any tusks," Kan says. "We can't prove they are poachers. But we'll report them to the authorities. When they make a move, the local rangers will stop them."

"I hope so," Alana says.

You do too. You may not have accomplished as much as you'd hoped for today, but you do feel like there's a chance you've made a difference.

THE END

To read another adventure, turn to page 9.
To learn more about endangered species, turn to page 101.

Tracking armed poachers sounds dangerous. You decide to play it safe and stick with collaring elephants. Ko and Win quickly pick up the tracks left behind by the elephants. You follow them through the rice field, across a deep, muddy stream, and into the woods. Mosquitos swarm you, and you get scratched up by thorny bushes. You drink your supply of water and are still thirsty. You stop to eat, but you drop your protein bar in the mud.

Turn the page.

Tracking endangered species often means going deep into the wilderness.

Eventually, dusk comes, and Ko shrugs his shoulders. "No elephants," he says in English.

"Tracking elephants is hard," Kan says. "Even when you have two of the best mahouts around helping you."

"Let's get back to the lab," Alana says. "I'm wiped out."

"That makes two of us," you say. You're tired and disappointed. But tomorrow is a new day. You'll try again then.

THE END

To read another adventure, turn to page 9.
To learn more about endangered species, turn to page 101.

"You there!" Charlie shouts. "We'd like to talk to you!"

The men look confused, and Charlie repeats himself in Burmese. The men exchange a glance, trying to make up their minds about what to do. Finally one of them comes up.

While Charlie and the men speak in Burmese, you glance into the Land Cruiser. The guns are there on the rack. There are maps on the floor and a cell phone on the dashboard. A pen and crumpled papers lie on the floor.

The men get back into their vehicle, and you get into Charlie's jeep.

"They say they are just visitors," Charlie says.

Maybe that's true. They may not be poachers. But as you leave the village, you see a flash of headlights behind you.

Turn the page.

"They're following us," Alana says.

Your stomach drops as Charlie hits the gas, and you go bouncing over the rough road at top speed. Dust kicks into the air behind you. Charlie sideswipes a tree on a tight turn. Suddenly, a gunshot rings out in the night. Just like with the charging elephant, Charlie stays calm. When he gets out of the woods and onto the paved road, he goes even faster. You look back.

"They're gone," you report.

"I have a feeling we'll see them again," Charlie says.

You have a sinking feeling he's right.

THE END

To read another adventure, turn to page 9.
To learn more about endangered species, turn to page 101.

You wait until the Land Cruiser is out of the village before you start to drive. You follow them with the headlights off—you almost run off the road twice. Eventually, you see the Land Cruiser parked in the bushes off the side of the road. You park 100 yards away and sneak closer. You creep into the forest, following their tracks.

Turn the page.

Ivory tusks are valuable because they can be made into many useful or decorative items.

You get close enough that you can hear the men talking. They are speaking Burmese, so you can't understand them. You peer into the darkness and see them hiding down in the tall grass. Charlie listens to their conversation, then signals for you all to follow him back to the road. Alana takes photos of their vehicle. Then you run back to the jeep.

As you drive back to the lab, Charlie explains that the men were talking about poaching an elephant. Elephants are known to travel through that area on their way to the stream in the mornings.

"We should stop them!" you say.

Charlie shakes his head. "It's too dangerous. We'll let the rangers deal with them."

Back at the lab, Charlie calls the rangers and emails them Alana's photos. They tell Charlie that they are on their way.

"The men will be arrested by daybreak," Charlie tells you with confidence.

THE END

To read another adventure, turn to page 9.
To learn more about endangered species, turn to page 101.

CHAPTER 3

SAVING THE SCIMITAR-HORNED ORYX

Scimitar-horned oryxes are desert antelope that have been extinct in the wild since the mid-1980s. But now scientists are introducing them back into their natural habitat in the grasslands of Chad. You want nothing more than to see the beauty of these animals up close. You've only seen photos.

"Let's go to Africa," you say to Alana. She readily agrees.

Your flight takes 33 hours, including layovers. When you touch down at the N'Djamena International Airport, you feel like you've traveled a million miles from home. But your journey is just beginning.

Turn the page.

You and Alana rent a little hatchback. You drive toward the small city of Ati, where you'll meet the other scientists.

It's a five-and-a-half-hour journey, and it's hot. The car has no air conditioning, so you drive with the windows down. The air whips through and cools you down a little. It's the middle of July. It's 95 degrees today without a cloud in sight. But it's the beginning of the rainy season, and you know the rain can come at any time.

At last, you arrive in the town. You are dusty from having the windows down. You pull up to a low, concrete house. As you get out of the car and stretch your achy legs, a man and woman come out to meet you. They are dressed in shorts and button-up shirts. The woman introduces herself as Issa. The man is Mathew. They invite you inside their home to discuss the project.

"The oryxes have been bred in captivity in Abu Dhabi," Issa says, while Mathew pours you and Alana glasses of lemonade. "A load of them are arriving tomorrow. We'll be taking them into the Ouadi Rimé-Ouadi Achim Game Reserve, just north of here."

The Reserve is massive—about the size of Scotland. When the oryxes are delivered, you'll truck them up to the grassland region for release.

"We already have a couple dozen oryxes that we released in recent months," Issa says. "Earlier today, we were monitoring them and identified a possible problem. So you can have your choice tomorrow. You can go with me into the grasslands with the new animals or stay here with Mathew to track the existing herd."

To go into the field with Issa, turn to page 46.

To monitor the oryxes from here with Mathew, turn to page 48.

45

You're eager to go into the field. The next day, you, Issa, and Alana pile into a big, rugged 4x4 and drive north into the reserve. At first, you're on a rough road, but the road gradually fades, and then you're bouncing over grasslands. Issa steers confidently but carefully. The afternoon sun pounds down, but a bank of clouds has formed on the horizon. An afternoon rain would be a nice break from the heat.

You arrive at a wide, temporary pen holding 12 scimitar-horned oryxes. You knew their horns were big, but the sight of them up close is breathtaking. Each horn is at least three feet long, curved back over the animal's body. A crew of half a dozen people are waiting for you. They are the scientists from Abu Dhabi who have been raising the oryxes.

Scimitar-horned oryxes

At one end of the pen is a small loading area, where the animals are prepped to be released. Issa turns to you with a big smile.

"I love this part of the job," she says. "Do you want to attach the collar or comfort the animals?"

To attach the collar, turn to page 50.
To comfort the oryxes, turn to page 52.

You're curious about the GPS tracking data setup. So after Issa drives off with Alana, you and Mathew head back inside the house. It's more of a combination house and lab. A small room off the kitchen holds a table with a computer with two large monitors. Maps are pinned to the walls, including a large one of the entire reserve.

Mathew pulls up a crude-looking outline of the reserve on one of the monitors and begins to zoom in on a particular area. You can see several dots representing tagged oryxes. He updates the feed, and you can see that several of the dots have moved.

"This group is really on the move," he says, pointing to a cluster of dots.

"Are they running away from a predator?" you ask.

"Could be," he replies. "We better get out there. You know how to ride a motorcycle?"

"Sort of," you say. You used to ride on your grandparents' farm when you were younger.

"Good enough," Mathew says.

Behind the house, Mathew pulls a blue tarp aside, revealing two filthy dirt bikes. He spends two minutes telling you how to work the controls, and then you're off. You ride across the grasslands with bugs and dust hitting your face. Mathew points to a dust cloud up ahead and turns in that direction. You follow.

As you get closer, you see people in a truck. Some of the men have rifles. They see you and take off. These people are not part of your group. They shouldn't be here.

Mathew drops back close to you and yells, "Poachers!"

To call the rangers, turn to page 54.
To follow the poachers, turn to page 65.

You didn't come here to watch other people do the work. You decide to put the collars on the animals. Issa and Alana step to either side of the loading pen as an oryx is led in. The women put on gloves, and Issa drapes a white towel over the nervous animal's face. Alana pats its flank and speaks softly to it.

One of the Abu Dhabi scientists hands you a canvas-sheathed collar with a small box attached—the GPS computer. You reach toward the oryx and wrap the collar around its neck. As you hold the clasp in place with one hand, the scientist helps you tighten the collar.

All the while, Alana whispers, "That a boy . . . good boy . . . you're doing fine . . ."

Finally, you give the collar a tug to make sure it is secure. Then you all step back, and Issa removes the towel.

The oryx bolts out of the gate, running and bucking over the grass. It butts its huge horns in the air, runs some more, and then stops. It looks around at its new surroundings. You repeat the process with 11 more oryxes.

When you've collared all of the animals, Issa tells you that some of the scientists are going to follow the oryxes released today to observe how they socialize with the rest of the herd.

"There's also a watering hole nearby that I like to check in on when I'm out this far," she says. "If it's not too dry, the oryxes might be gathered there. Sometimes you can watch a group in action. Would you like to observe one of the oryxes we just collared or come with me to the watering hole?"

To tail an oryx you released today, turn to page 55.
To check out the watering hole, turn to page 57.

Your heart leaps at the idea of comforting these beautiful creatures. Your job is to keep the oryx from getting antsy and starting to buck or thrash. With those long horns, someone could get seriously hurt. One of the scientists from Abu Dhabi hands you a white towel.

"Here, put this over its eyes," she says. "And keep it tight. If he can't see, he won't be stressed when we attach the collar."

You cover the oryx's eyes with the towel while Issa coos gently to it. Alana and another scientist work quickly to wrap a collar with a GPS monitor around its neck. Alana drops a screwdriver and exclaims, "Oh, shoot."

As the tool hits the ground, the muscles in the oryx's neck flex under your fingers. It starts to move forward and back nervously. It could start thrashing any second.

A scimitar-horned oryx GPS tracking collar

Suddenly one of the scientists behind you says sharply, "Pull that back!"

Is she talking to you? Should you remove the towel?

To remove the towel, turn to page 60.

To hold steady, turn to page 62.

"Let's call the ranger," you say.

"Good idea," Mathew says. He gets on his radio and makes the call.

While you're waiting for the ranger, you search for evidence. Did the poachers get any of the oryxes? Why were the oryxes here anyway? Mathew points at some shrubs with bite marks. The oryxes have been feeding on them.

As the sun sets, you see several oryxes walk out of the hills. They take shelter in a stand of acacia trees—a rare cool spot in the desert.

You record the information about the shrubs and acacia trees. This will be valuable information for the research team. Though the poachers got away, this is a small victory.

THE END

To read another adventure, turn to page 9.
To learn more about endangered species, turn to page 101.

After putting on its collar and watching that first oryx run across the land, you feel sort of attached to him.

"Let's watch that first guy," you say.

You, Alana, and Issa pile back into the 4x4 and follow the oryx from a couple hundred yards back. It is now walking along the grassland. After a time, it begins to gallop again. Issa tracks it using GPS on her phone.

Later that afternoon, you catch up to the animal as it is meeting the rest of the herd. It approaches the group, and another male challenges it. They fight, butting each other with their massive horns.

"We have to stop them," you say. You figure your oryx is at a disadvantage since it's never lived in the wild before.

Turn the page.

But Issa says, "Just watch."

The two males battle for about 10 minutes. They clash so hard their horns clack like a bat hitting a baseball. Eventually, the two seem to grow tired and let up. They all graze together in the dusk as a light rain begins to fall. You know it will get heavy soon. Issa turns the truck around.

"We did good today," Issa says, as you bounce over the rutted grassland. "And tomorrow we'll do more."

The rain begins to fall harder, soaking you in the open 4x4. It feels refreshing. You shut your eyes and picture the oryx again. You'll do more for these animals tomorrow, yes. But that will always be your first oryx.

THE END

To read another adventure, turn to page 9.
To learn more about endangered species, turn to page 101.

Issa drives south, back toward the house. The sky grows dark, and a light rain begins to fall. Then it grows heavy. You are getting drenched in the open 4x4. It's refreshing at first, but after a while you just feel gross.

Despite the rain, when you arrive at the watering hole, you find that it's empty. The current rainfall has created only a small stream of water over the dry, cracked ground.

"That's what I was afraid of," Issa says. "The dry season has been really bad this year."

The rainy season is just beginning. But it will be a long time before this watering hole gets enough water to support the oryxes in the reserve—if it ever does.

"We have to help if we want this herd to keep growing," she says. "We need to head back to town for supplies."

Turn the page.

Night falls as you drive back. Once you're in cell-phone range, Issa calls Mathew. She needs the tank truck filled with water.

In the morning, you and Issa take the 4x4 to a farming supply store and buy four large metal troughs. The sun is hot again, and there is no rain expected today as you drive back out into the reserve. Alana and Mathew follow you and Issa in the tank truck.

At the watering hole, you unload the big tubs and set them up along its dry edge. Then Mathew moves the tank truck closer. You and Alana pull the wide hose off and point it into the first trough. Issa turns on the water. It doesn't take long to get all four troughs full. Hopefully the oryxes will come and drink. And your team can keep these troughs full instead of the water being sucked into the dry earth.

It is a struggle for many animals to find watering holes in the dry desert.

As you're about to leave, you see movement in the distance. You wait. An oryx ambles closer. Another one appears behind it at the top of the rise. Then another. As you watch, all three oryxes approach the troughs and begin to drink. It feels good knowing you've helped make a difference.

THE END

To read another adventure, turn to page 9.
To learn more about endangered species, turn to page 101.

You better act quickly. You remove the towel from the oryx's face. As soon as you do, its eyes dart around. It starts to thrash and buck inside the tight wooden loading pen. Its long horns whip through the air. Suddenly, you're gashed under the arm. You cry out and fall back into the dirt.

The oryx keeps bucking and rearing its head. Everyone else steps away to keep safe, but the oryx is going to hurt itself. Issa quickly puts together a large syringe. She reaches over the side of the pen, injects the oryx, and jumps back.

Within seconds, the oryx calms down. Slobber is dripping from its mouth. Its hind legs quiver, then fold up. In moments, it is out cold on the ground.

"Why did you take the towel off?" Issa asks you. "You have to leave it on—that's how they stay calm."

"Someone said pull it back," you say defensively. "I was just doing what I was told!"

"I was talking about the clasp on the collar," says a scientist behind you. She shakes her head.

"Are you okay?" Alana asks.

The side of your shirt is dark with blood.

"I'm not sure," you groan.

Issa sighs. "We need to get you back to the house," she says.

You sit up front on the long drive back to the house. With each bump on the road, you moan in pain. The bleeding has slowed, but the wound will need to be treated. You hope that tomorrow you'll be able to go back out and prove your worth.

THE END

To read another adventure, turn to page 9.
To learn more about endangered species, turn to page 101.

The oryx is already jumpy. Your gut tells you not to remove the towel. You keep it on and say a few calming words to the animal.

"Pull it back," the same person says again. You can't turn back to look at her, but you see Alana in front of you giving the GPS collar a tug. "There it is," the woman behind you says.

Alana gets the holes to line up with the screws and quickly tightens down the hex nuts on the collar. The oryx is still jumpy, but you're almost ready to let it go.

Just hold on, you think.

Suddenly the oryx rears back. You swing your head out of the way just in time to avoid being stabbed by its horn. It gives a deep, distressed grumble, but you hold steady with the towel.

Alana steps back. "All set!" she says.

Turn the page.

Issa tugs on the collar to make sure it's secure, then opens the front of the gate. You remove the towel, and the oryx bolts out into the field. Everyone cheers.

"Look at it go!" you say.

The oryx runs up a rise, then stops to look back on you. From this distance, it's just a silhouette against the sun. The animal looks calm. To you, it looks like a symbol of the success yet to come. Thanks to the hard work of scientists like you, the oryx herd will continue to grow and thrive.

THE END

To read another adventure, turn to page 9.
To learn more about endangered species, turn to page 101.

You trail the poachers at a distance, hoping they don't notice you following. They drive into the hills and then into a canyon. You pull over and cut your motors and wait. You can't see the men, but soon you see campfire smoke rising from the canyon.

Mathew gets on his radio and calls a park ranger. The ranger will assemble a team of four and head out here right away. You and Mathew ride down and wait for them at the foot of the hills. That way you won't be caught alone by the armed men.

You sit on a rock and throw stones to kill time. The rain begins to fall hard, but you don't have any shelter. You don't even have a rain jacket. A truck approaches on the road, and you stand up to greet them, but Mathew tells you to get back.

Turn the page.

"They're not the rangers," Mathew whispers.

You wheel the bikes behind a giant red boulder and wait, hoping whoever it is didn't see you. Their headlights sweep across the boulder and pause. You hear men get out of the truck. They speak to each other in low voices. The men stay there for a long time—too long. You think of the tire tracks your motorcycles left. Did they notice them?

Finally the people pile back into the truck and head uphill. You realize they're going to join the poachers you followed.

"Do you think they knew we are here?" you ask Mathew.

"Maybe," he says. "We might not be safe here."

To run away, turn to page 69.
To keep waiting for the rangers, turn to page 70.

"Let's get out of here," you say.

You push the bikes out from behind the boulder and fire them up. Just as you do, two sets of headlights appear up on the hill.

"Here they come!" Mathew shouts. "Follow me!"

He hits the throttle and rips down the road. You are right behind him. You're still a little shaky on the motorcycle, but you're getting the hang of it. The rain isn't helping though. It pelts your face, making it hard to see. It makes the road slick and dangerous. Luckily the bikes are quicker than the poachers' trucks, and you cover some distance quickly. But each time you look back, you see that they're still on your trail.

You keep riding. Soon the road fades and you are riding over bumpy, muddy land.

You can't go as fast. The trucks gain on you. You hear gunshots behind you. You reach a stretch of hard desert. On the firm surface, you're able to gain speed again. The rain slows down, and you are riding directly into the sun when it breaks over the horizon at dawn.

You chance a look back. The trucks are gone.

"We lost them!" you yell.

Mathew gives you the thumbs up. You ride back to the house, your heart still pumping hard from the chase. You breathe a sigh of relief, but now you know that those poachers are out there. You will do everything you can to stop them. After a nice long nap, of course.

THE END

To read another adventure, turn to page 9.
To learn more about endangered species, turn to page 101.

"The rangers will be here soon," Mathew says to you. "Let's hold tight."

To be on the safe side, you decide to move down the road a bit to hide in a different spot. It was a good thing you did. The poachers drive back down and check your previous spot behind the boulder. Then they briefly search the area and head back up the hill. It's clear the poachers knew you were there.

Soon two trucks come up from the south. Mathew steps out to greet the rangers. They talk briefly, and then they head up the hill. You and Mathew stay behind. Neither one of you are armed, and things could get dangerous.

As you wait, you hear a couple gunshots in the distance. Soon the rangers come back down the hill.

The poachers are in handcuffs in the back of their truck. You feel a chill go down your neck. But you succeeded. You helped stop the poachers.

THE END

To read another adventure, turn to page 9.
To learn more about endangered species, turn to page 101.

CHAPTER 4

FROGS IN PANAMA

Frogs have always been your favorite animals. Your little cousin Martin shares your enthusiasm. You're guessing from Alana's earrings that they're her favorite too. You and Alana pack your bags for Panama City to help.

At the research center there, you meet a researcher named Dr. Mirabella Shayne. She is an expert on the chytrid fungus. It is killing off frogs in Panama and around the world.

"Welcome," Dr. Shayne says, shaking your hands. "You can call me Mirabella."

Mirabella's fingernails have dirt under them. Her boots and jeans are muddy. It's as if she barely took time away from her work in the jungle to meet you, and she's ready to jump back in.

Turn the page.

You don't blame her. The chytrid fungus is spreading at an alarming rate. The fungus infects frogs' skin, which affects their ability to breathe through their skin and absorb important nutrients. The fungus begins to eat away at the skin and eventually leads to a heart attack, killing the frog. The disease has caused dramatic population declines in at least 501 amphibian species all over the world, including 90 extinctions, over the past 50 years. Eight of those species were from Panama. There are 52 more species of frogs there that have had more than a 90 percent drop in population.

"Losing amphibians is harmful to the environment," Mirabella tells you. "Frogs, newts, and toads play an important role in maintaining healthy ecosystems. For example, frogs eat insects that spread disease. They also provide food for birds and other animals."

"Not only that," she adds, sitting on the edge of the table, "secretions from frogs' skin may be used to develop medicines. If frogs die off, we'll lose the ability to treat untold numbers of diseases and illnesses."

"What do we do first?" you ask.

"We have a population of frogs we've been treating in our lab," Mirabella explains. "We plan to do one last round of testing tomorrow. After that, we'll take them into the forest and release them."

"Sounds great," Alana says.

I wish my cousin Martin you could be here, you think.

That evening, the three of you have dinner together at a café in town. Just as you're finishing up, Mirabella gets a call on her cell.

Turn the page.

When she hangs up, she tells you that some biologists working in a remote part of the Amazon Rain Forest in Peru have rescued a bunch of tadpoles from a pond where frogs were dying. This could be key to your research. They found a pilot of a firefighter helicopter who is willing to drop off the tadpoles on his way to a fire in Colombia. But the pilot can't come all the way to Panama City. He'll have to drop off the tadpoles in a remote part of the jungle. Someone has to drive out to meet him and get the tadpoles.

"It looks like we have a choice to make," Mirabella says.

To test the frogs in the lab, go to the next page.
To get the tadpoles in the jungle, turn to page 81.

You're not familiar with this area yet. You decide to work in the lab, where your training can do the most good. The next morning, you meet Alana and Mirabella there.

The frogs are in a large aquarium. Known as golden frogs, they are a buttery color with black spots. They are beautiful and move gracefully. Martin would love this.

You open the top and reach in to grab one of the frogs, but it hops away. Alana and Mirabella give you some friendly teasing. But the next frog you go for leaps right into your waiting hands. You hold it gently while Alana rubs a cotton swab across its back. Then she smears the swab onto a microscope slide.

Turn the page.

You place the slide under the microscope. You are looking for signs of the chytrid fungus. Mirabella has shown you how to see it in the slides. As you look, you identify a lot of bacteria and other living cells squirming around on there. But you don't see any sign of the fungus. You test several more frogs throughout the morning, and they all come up negative.

"The treatment you've been giving them seems to have been successful," Alana says to Mirabella.

"Yes, it's time to let them go," Mirabella says. "We want to see if they will breed new generations of frogs that have the same resistance to the fungus. We'll track these frogs with these." She reaches into a plastic tub and pulls out a tiny GPS transmitter fitted to a belt that goes around the frogs' middle.

Turn the page.

Each frog will be painted with a mark that glows under UV light. That way, scientists can identify the frogs later on. The three of you start marking the frogs in the aquarium and fitting them with GPS transmitter belts.

Once all of the frogs are marked, Mirabella and Alana go to get a Jeep so you can take them into the forest. She asks you to load the frogs into a cooler. You're alone with the frogs. You think again of Martin, who has been very sick. You would love to cheer him up. You could care for this little guy until it's time to go home and show Martin.

To pocket one of the frogs to take home to Martin, turn to page 85.

To just load the frogs into the cooler, turn to page 87.

Seeing a firefighter helicopter in the rain forest is an adventure you can't pass up. You tell Mirabella you're in for the trip. You can tell she's excited too.

Mirabella drives the Jeep through the forest along a firm dirt road. But as night falls, the road gets rougher. Soon you're wobbling over rocks and tree trunks and angling through ravines. Mirabella stops to let some air out of the tires.

"This will lower the air pressure and makes the tires softer," she explains. "The tires will grip the ground better."

Insects keep flying in your face, and they're not just little mosquitos. Some of them are the size of wadded-up notebook paper. You're covered in bug bites by the time you reach a clearing. It looks wide enough to land a helicopter. Sure enough, 20 minutes later, you hear the thumping blades.

Turn the page.

The Jeep's headlights light up the clearing. As the helicopter lowers, the trees ripple from the wind. Its engine and thwacking blades drown out the insects and every thought in your head. Two firefighters climb out carrying coolers. You look inside the first cooler—it's full of water and dozens of squirming tadpoles. The firefighters climb back into the helicopter, and you wave as they lift off. Suddenly, it is quiet. Even the insects are silent for now.

You load the two coolers into the back of the Jeep, and Mirabella turns the car around. A thin rain begins to fall. Unfortunately, the Jeep has no roof.

"There's a pond just north of here that I want to check out," Mirabella says. "Some of the frogs we released have made a home there. We tracked them with GPS."

Turn the page.

"Shouldn't we get these tadpoles back?" Alana asks.

You agree they probably need fresh water and nutrition. You're also cold, wet, and tired. It's almost morning.

"They'll be fine if we're quick," Mirabella says. "But I'll leave it up to you. You two have already had a long day."

To go to the pond, turn to page 90.
To go straight back to the lab, turn to page 93.

Nobody will notice one missing frog. And you know you can transport it home safely. Maybe Martin will start to feel better when he sees it. You stick your head into the hallway to make sure nobody is coming. The coast is clear, so you put your hand into the aquarium and snatch one. You drop it into a small container with some damp towels for moisture and slip that into the pocket of your coat.

You walk down the hall toward the office where your bag is so you can stash the frog inside. You are just pulling the box out of your pocket when you hear a voice behind you.

"What are you doing?" Mirabella says.

You turn around. Guilt is written all over your face. "I know it's wrong," you say. "But I didn't think it would really hurt anything."

Turn the page.

"Transporting invasive species is a large part of how we got into this mess!" Mirabella says. She looks furious.

"I'm sorry," you say. "I'll put it back."

But Mirabella shakes her head. "I can't have you on this project," she says. "I can't trust you. Leave now."

It should have been an amazing day. But instead of driving into the forest to release golden frogs to repopulate their species with a resistance to chytrid fungus, you spend the afternoon filling out paperwork. You are officially removed from the project, and by morning you find yourself back at the airport. You're going home, and your career is over.

THE END

To read another adventure, turn to page 9.
To learn more about endangered species, turn to page 101.

Martin would love his own golden frog, of course. Who wouldn't? But you know stealing is wrong. And moving species can cause damage to new habitats.

You pour a couple gallons of water into a long white cooler. Then you start placing the frogs inside. Alana comes back into the lab and helps you finish up. You both carry the cooler out to the parking lot, where Mirabella is waiting in a Jeep.

Mirabella drives you several hours into the forest, to a place where the river curves and widens into a broad pond. You're almost there when you hear a loud crack. Your head jerks forward, hitting the dashboard.

"What happened?" Alana says from the back seat.

Turn the page.

"We hit a big rock," Mirabella says.

You all get out to inspect the Jeep. The axle is broken. You won't be driving this anymore today.

Mirabella radios back to the lab for help. You realize that you're only a few miles from the pond. You and Alana decide to carry the cooler the rest of the way. You both grab a handle and follow Mirabella along the road. Soon, she takes you on a shortcut through the underbrush. She slashes at the branches and grasses with a big knife she grabbed from the Jeep.

The pond is shimmering green in the afternoon sun. You and Alana set the cooler down in the grass. Mirabella kneels in the mud to open it. One by one, you take the frogs out and set them near the water. You watch as they sit still, taking in their new environment, then hop cautiously into the water.

That night, another scientist picks you up and drives you back to the lab. Once you get back, you watch the frogs move around their new home through the GPS transmitters. You feel confident that your hard work will pay off. Maybe future generations of frogs will be resistant to chytrid.

THE END

To read another adventure, turn to page 9.
To learn more about endangered species, turn to page 101.

Yes, you're exhausted, the bugs are biting, and you're shivering cold. But there's a reason for all of that—you're here to help with the frog project.

"Let's do it," you say.

Mirabella drives the Jeep north through a swamp. Then she climbs onto another road hidden in the brush. She really knows this forest. You're whizzing along the road, the trees and brush blurring past. In half an hour, Mirabella stops the Jeep in another swampy area. You climb out and walk through the mud. It sucks at your boots. Finally, just as the morning sun is starting to glow in the trees above you, you take a step—not into mud but into nice, clear water.

The pond is not big—maybe 50 yards across. But it's clear. You can hear water running over rocks from somewhere.

Mirabella leads you to a spring that feeds the pond. At your feet, a dozen frogs float dead in the water. A few more lie in the mud.

"Oh, no," you say. "What happened?"

"Wait," Alana says. "They don't have monitors on them."

Turn the page.

A water frog lies dead, most likely killed by the chytrid fungus.

"No, these are not our frogs," Mirabella says.

"Are you sure your frogs are here?" you ask.

"Somewhere," she says.

"We better get back to those tadpoles," Alana says. "They've been in those coolers a long time."

"You're right," Mirabella says. "Still, we're going to have to test the frogs in this pond soon. If we don't do it today, we'll have to come all the way out here again."

You think of how long and hard the journey was. It would be nice to get the testing done now. It seems like Mirabella wants to keep looking, but you all know it's a risk.

To hurry back to the tadpoles, turn to page 96.
To keep looking for the tagged frogs, turn to page 98.

"Let's get back to the lab," you suggest. "We know the frogs are out here somewhere, and if we take too long, the tadpoles could die."

Mirabella reluctantly agrees and drives you back. It is midmorning when you pull into the lot and carry the two coolers into the lab. Mirabella directs you toward a large, clean aquarium. She begins filling it with water and moss. There are already large rocks and a filter inside, which she turns on.

As you load the tadpoles into the aquarium, you study them. Mirabella believes they are a species of frog that is nearly extinct. If you have enough of them, you may be able to help grow the species so that it's less threatened. You try to count them, but there are too many and they move too quickly.

Turn the page.

Over several days, the tadpoles transform. They grow legs, and their tales shrink. One day, you walk into the lab, and you have an aquarium full of hopping frogs. You move some into a separate aquarium, injecting them with a small amount of chytrid fungus. Doing this should build up their immunity to the fungus.

A yellow poison dart frog in an aquarium

A couple hours later, you apply a purple bacteria called *J. lividum* that fights chytrid. This is taken from other species of frogs that are not affected by the fungus. You hope it will help these frogs similarly become immune.

The next week, you inject the same frogs again with chytrid. This time, it's clear that the fungus does not affect them.

"Success!" Alana says.

Mirabella has a big smile on her face. You do too. You have helped build up these frogs' immunity to the fungus. They are ready to go back into the wild.

THE END

To read another adventure, turn to page 9.
To learn more about endangered species, turn to page 101.

"We better hurry back," you say. "But if we can figure out what happened to these frogs, maybe we can prevent it from happening again. Do you think we have time to take some of them to study?"

"Good idea," Mirabella says.

Nobody has a container, so you pull out the bottom of your shirt to make a sort of basket. Then you start scooping up the dead frogs. Mirabella and Alana do the same. You walk carefully through the swamp back to the Jeep and place them in the trunk next to the coolers full of tadpoles.

Mirabella quickly steers through the rainforest. You reach the lab by lunchtime. You run inside to grab a bucket and carry it back out to the Jeep. Alana loads it up with dead frogs. You carry the frogs and coolers inside.

That afternoon, after transferring the tadpoles to a tank, you turn your attention to the dead frogs. You swab their backs to get a sample, then look at it under a microscope. You recognize the floating spores—these frogs died of chytrid fungus.

"So we know these frogs had chytrid," Mirabella says. "But we still don't know how our treated frogs are doing."

You check the GPS. It appears that many of them are still at that pond. Are they okay? You won't know until you go back out and check on them. You'll continue to test and tag more frogs. Little by little, you are helping to unravel the mystery of chytrid. There's a lot of work to do, but you can see a light at the end of the tunnel.

THE END

To read another adventure, turn to page 9.
To learn more about endangered species, turn to page 101.

"We're here now," you say. "We should find those tagged frogs."

"Let's be fast," Mirabella says.

On the opposite side of the pond, a stream leads out. It will meet up with other streams and eventually make its way to the Amazon River. You want to reach the beginning of the stream, so the three of you trudge through the mud and swarming bugs. Fish dart through the water. Something large makes splashes. The sun bakes you. It is hard to move quickly.

Finally you reach the stream and see the first GPS-tagged frog. It's hiding between some rocks and brush near where the water starts to rush faster. You catch it, and Mirabella wipes its back with a cotton swab. She slips the swab into a baggie. Alana finds another one and Mirabella repeats the process. Then you find another.

In all, you test eight frogs. You're feeling great as you drive back to the lab—you have accomplished a lot in the last 24 hours! But when you unload the tadpoles at the lab, many of them are floating dead in the water.

"Didn't they have enough oxygen?" Alana asks.

"Most likely they didn't have enough food," Mirabella says. "Let's move fast."

You load the remaining tadpoles into an aquarium as fast as you can. Mirabella adds moss to the tank, and you watch as many of the tadpoles gobble at it. You lost a lot of them, but you saved many. You hope it's enough to get conclusive results from your tests. And for them to reproduce.

THE END

To read another adventure, turn to page 9.
To learn more about endangered species, turn to page 101.

CHAPTER 5

ENDANGERED SPECIES

All over the world, plant and animals species are declining at an alarming rate. Since humans have been on this planet, the biomass of wild animals, or total amount of each species, has decreased by 82 percent.

From the tiniest insects to mighty elephants, about 1 million species of plants and animals are facing extinction. Insect populations are going down. Forty percent of amphibians are at risk of extinction. Coral reefs are dying. Rain forests are being cut down. Since the 1970s, North America has lost about one-third of all wild birds.

Humans are the main reason for this. We have turned about 75 percent of all of Earth's land into farm fields or concrete cityscapes or made other big changes.

Humans have altered two-thirds of the oceans and seas with fish farms, shipping routes, and other projects. We use about three-quarters of rivers and lakes for raising crops or livestock. These changes leave little habitat for animals.

We also are damaging species through poaching, pollution, burning fossil fuels, and moving species to different habitats. Almost 100 years ago, humans moved frogs that had chytrid fungus on them into new habitats. Those frogs weren't harmed by the chytrid, but the frogs they came into contact with were.

The survival of other species is very important for human life on Earth. All animal life on the planet is dependent on each other. Losing species seriously threatens our health and our way of life.

The variety of plant and animal life on Earth is called biodiversity. Strong biodiversity is critical to regulating the climate. It also protects coasts from erosion and damage. Plant and animal species also provide food, fresh water, medicines, fuel, fertile soils, building materials, and air to breathe.

The relationship between climate change and declining biodiversity is a vicious cycle. Climate change makes habitats less livable for all sorts of living things. Species begin to die out, including plants that store carbon dioxide. Warmer oceans, too, are less capable of storing carbon. That means more carbon is stored in the atmosphere. And, in turn, more carbon in the atmosphere leads to rising temperatures. That leads to further climate change.

That's why scientists all over the world are fighting so hard to save animal and plant species. Our very survival depends on it.

TRACKING ENDANGERED ANIMALS

Take a look at where the activities you just learned about are taking place. These are just a handful of the more than 30,000 species of endangered animals on the planet.

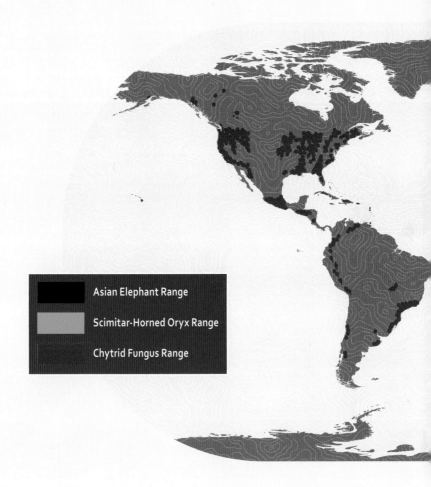

Asian Elephant Range

Scimitar-Horned Oryx Range

Chytrid Fungus Range

GLOSSARY

amphibian (am-FI-bee-uhn)—a cold-blooded animal with a backbone; amphibians live in water when young and can live on land as adults

biologist (by-AH-luh-jist)—a scientist who studies living things

biomass (BY-oh-mass)—the total quantity of living organisms of an animal or plant species

breed (BREED)—to mate and produce young

captivity (kap-TIV-ih-tee)—when an animal is kept in a zoo or wildlife park

conservation (kon-sur-VAY-shuhn)—the protection of animals and plants

ecosystem (EE-koh-sis-tuhm)—a group of animals and plants that work together with their surroundings

endangered (in-DAYN-juhrd)—at risk of dying out

expedition (ek-spuh-DI-shuhn)— a journey made for a particular reason

extinct (ik-STINGKT)—no longer living; an extinct animal is one that has died out, with no more of its kind

fungus (FUHN-guhs)—a living thing similar to a plant, but without flowers, leaves, or green coloring

GPS (gee-pee-ESS)—an electronic tool that uses satellites to find the location of objects; GPS stands for Global Positioning System

habitat (HAB-uh-tat)—the natural place and conditions in which a plant or animal lives

mahout (muh-HOUT)—a person who works with and tends to elephants

poacher (POHCH-ur)—a person who hunts or fishes illegally

species (SPEE-sheez)—a group of animals with similar features

syringe (suh-RINJ)—a tube with a plunger and a hollow needle used to inject medicine

tranquilizer (TRANG-kwul-lye-zur)—a drug that has a calming effect

tusks (TUHSKS)—very long, pointed teeth that stick out when the mouth is closed

OTHER PATHS TO EXPLORE

>>> Many threats to species are caused by humans, even though having diverse species is critical to life on Earth. Why do you think that is?

>>> Would you like to work as an endangered species scientist? What would be some of the rewards and drawbacks?

>>> Plants and animals are all connected in the circle of life. Think of your favorite animal. What other plants and animals would be affected if that animal was suddenly gone?

READ MORE

Braun, Eric. *Can You Save A Tropical Rain Forest? An Interactive Eco Adventure.* North Mankato, MN, Capstone Press, 2021.

Jenkins, Martin. *Under Threat: An Album of Endangered Animals.* Somerville, MA: Candlewick Press, 2019.

Perdew, Laura. *Biodiversity: Explore the Diversity of Life on Earth with Environmental Science Activities for Kids.* White River Junction, VT: Nomad Press, 2019.

INTERNET SITES

DK Find Out! Endangered Animals
dkfindout.com/us/more-find-out/special-events/
endangered-animals/

Smithsonian's National Zoo & Conservation Biology Institute
nationalzoo.si.edu

Endangered Animals Facts for Kids
activewild.com/endangered-animals-facts-for-kids/

INDEX